A Boy
in the Doghouse

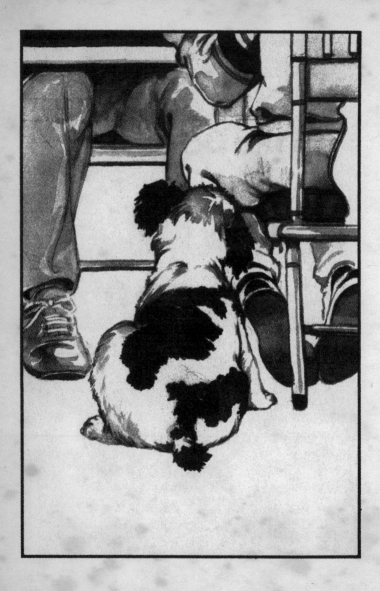

A Boy
in the Doghouse

Betsy Duffey

illustrated by Leslie Morrill

A TRUMPET CLUB SPECIAL EDITION

Published by The Trumpet Club
666 Fifth Avenue, New York, New York 10103

Text copyright © 1991 by Betsy Duffey
Illustrations copyright © 1991 by Leslie Morrill

ISBN 0-440-84864-4

This edition published by arrangement with
Simon and Schuster Books for Young Readers, a
division of Simon & Schuster, Inc.

Designed by Vicki Kalajian.

The illustrations were done in watercolor.

Printed in the United States of America
September 1992

1 3 5 7 9 10 8 6 4 2
CWO

For Scott

Contents

A Boy
in the Doghouse

The Puddle Problem

ERF! ERF!

George's eyes blinked open. He looked over at his clock.

2:00 A.M.

ERF! ERF!

He lay in bed wide awake. From the back-yard came the barks of a lonely puppy.

ERF! ERF!

George said a prayer. "Please stop, Lucky. Please stop barking!"

ERF! ERF!

By now his mother and father might be awake. They would be angry about the bark-ing. Soon they would be on their way down-stairs.

1

ERF! ERF!

Mrs. Haines, the next-door neighbor, might wake up too. She would call George's parents and complain. She might even call the police.

ERF! ERF!

George couldn't stand it anymore. He jumped out of bed and ran downstairs, carrying his blanket.

When he got to the door he eased it open and slipped out into the backyard.

The air was cool. The grass was cold and wet on his bare feet.

ERF! ERF!

He hurried over to the doghouse.

"Quiet, boy," he whispered. "You've got to be quiet!"

Lucky licked George's face. His little body wiggled with delight.

ERRRF!

He barked one bark of happiness, then licked George some more.

"Quiet, boy! You've got to settle down."

George tried to make Lucky lie down. He

tried to cover him with the blanket, but Lucky grabbed the blanket in his teeth. He shook his head back and forth, playing tug-of-war.

"Cut it out," whispered George. "It's bedtime! You're supposed to go to sleep now!"

ERRRF!

George looked at the back of his house. He could see his parents' bedroom window. The lights had not come on.

George had to find a way to make Lucky stop barking.

He knelt down and began to scratch Lucky behind the ears.

Lucky stopped shaking the blanket.

George petted his head and scratched him under the chin.

Lucky dropped the blanket and sat back on his hind legs.

Now George rubbed his back and behind his ears.

Lucky lay down all the way, and his eyes began to close.

"Good dog," said George softly. "Good dog."

George's arm began to ache at the shoulder from so much petting, but he didn't dare stop. Every time he stopped, Lucky's eyes would pop open again.

He wondered if Lucky would ever go to sleep. When morning came, would he still be here in the doghouse, petting Lucky?

His parents would not be pleased to find George sleeping in the doghouse. He *must* not fall asleep.

He leaned back against the rough wood on the inside of the doghouse and looked down at Lucky lying beside him.

George had had Lucky for only one week. He had great plans for him. He would teach him wonderful tricks—to walk on his hind legs, to come when he was called, to say his prayers. George planned to teach him to balance a dog biscuit on his nose like a dog that he had seen on television.

George planned to teach Lucky lots of

things. But first he had to work on the two most important things—not barking and not making puddles in the house.

If he couldn't teach him those two things pretty soon, Lucky would have to go.

His parents were losing patience with Lucky.

They had been angry when Lucky had chewed the corner off George's father's new briefcase.

They were not happy about the barking at night.

They were especially upset about the puddles.

New puppies make a lot of puddles. On the living room floor. On the kitchen floor. On the bedroom floor. Everywhere except outside.

Lucky had a puddle problem.

George's parents had given George one week to see if Lucky would work out. Tomorrow the week was up. So far Lucky had learned nothing.

George kept petting Lucky on the head.

He had wanted a dog for so long. When his

parents had finally said yes, George had wanted to be the perfect master.

He really loved Lucky. He would do anything for Lucky.

He always cleaned up the puddles and never scolded Lucky even once.

He gave him plenty of things to chew on. He never got mad when he chewed things up, even his baseball glove.

And now, here he was, sleeping with Lucky in his doghouse.

What more could a master do for a dog?

He put his head down next to Lucky's warm back.

Without stopping his petting he pulled the blanket up around him.

He hoped Lucky would start to learn soon.

Tomorrow was a new day.

Tomorrow he would train this dog.

The important thing now was to get Lucky sound asleep and get back to his own bed. The important thing was *not* to fall asleep in the doghouse.

He kept petting Lucky.

The last thing he remembered was the ache in his arm as he drifted off to sleep—in the dog-house.

Boy Training

Lucky snuggled comfortably under the blanket. The boy's head felt warm next to his back. He was almost asleep.

It had worked! He knew that if he barked long enough the boy would come out. Now he knew what to do at night—keep barking until the boy came out!

His new home was fine. Much better than the place he lived last week—THE POUND.

They didn't treat him very well at THE POUND. No one petted him even once. And all they gave him to eat was dry puppy food. Didn't they know about HAM?

He had watched his brother and sister puppies get chosen, one by one. He had sat back

and watched. He had not wanted to choose too
quickly. He had wanted to get the perfect new
home.

His sister had chosen the first person who
walked in. A middle-aged woman with *high
heels*. Lucky knew better than that. His mother
had taught him the importance of shoes. High
heels were bad news. Women in high heels did
not take dogs for walks.

His brother had chosen the second people who walked in. He had chosen a couple with a *baby*. Lucky knew better than that too. Babies meant tail pulling, ear chewing, and, worst of all, less attention for a dog.

Lucky had waited patiently. He would know when the perfect people came along.

Finally, when he had almost given up hope, he saw the boy. Right away he knew this was the one. He wasn't too clean. He looked like someone who would run in the grass and not worry about muddy footprints on his pants.

Lucky checked his shoes. Yes, they were just about worn out. The boy would be good for walks. Perfect. The boy was perfect!

He remembered his mother's instructions about how to get adopted. Hold tail up. Show spunk. No drooling.

He knew just what to do. Wag his tail like crazy and *wiggle*. She had said people can't resist a wiggling puppy. And he remembered— licking only, *no biting*.

It had worked! The boy had picked him out.

So here he was. A new home. A new dog-house. And a new boy to train. He would have to work fast. The boy had a lot to learn!

He would teach him to give him table scraps, and HAM. And not to snatch him up every time he made a little puddle.

Didn't the boy know that he had to make puddles?

After he had the boy trained, he would work on the man and woman.

He could already tell that the man liked him. The man had thrown his slipper at Lucky when he chewed on the briefcase. The man must have known how much better the slipper would taste!

The man was a little strange though. Every morning the man took him outside, put him down in the grass, and stared at him. What was he waiting for?

Then he would yell "Come, come!" and chase Lucky around the yard in his bathrobe. Didn't he know how ridiculous he looked?

What did "Come, come" mean anyway?

All in all his new home was okay. He would give them another day or two to learn.

He snuggled down again and closed his eyes. At least he had taught the boy one thing.

To sleep with him in the doghouse.

Tomorrow was a new day.

Tomorrow he would train this boy some more.

Lucky on the Loose

"George! Geeoorrge!"

George heard a voice in the distance. Far away. It was like a dream.

"Geeoorrge!"

He pulled his blanket around himself and stretched out his legs. His muscles were stiff. His feet hit something hard—the side of the doghouse.

Doghouse!

It all came back to him.

It was morning, and he was in Lucky's doghouse.

He looked around.

Lucky was gone. Lucky was on the loose.

Now what? He had to get back to his bedroom before his mother came looking for him. He had to find Lucky. He crawled out of the doghouse.

"There you are!" his mother called from the back door.

He was caught.

He didn't know what to say. He held his breath. He tried to think of an excuse for sleeping in the doghouse.

"You're up early!" his mother said. "You must have come out to look for Lucky."

George let out his breath.

"Get Lucky and come on in for breakfast," said his mother. She walked back into the house.

Relief! He wasn't in trouble.

He had to get Lucky. Where was Lucky anyway?

George looked around the backyard. He didn't see Lucky anywhere.

Had Lucky gone through the fence again?

Was he eating Mrs. Haines's Japanese dogwoods?

George ran around to the front yard. No sign of Lucky.

He thought about all the bad-dog stories that he had heard.

One time Jimmy Johnson's basset hound, Ernie, had been left alone in the house.

The Johnsons had gone shopping. They had not taken Ernie along. Ernie hated to be left behind.

While they were gone, Ernie got his revenge.

He went into Jimmy's father's closet and chewed shoes. The whole time that they were gone. Worse than that, he chewed only one shoe of each pair. Then he dragged the chewed shoes down to the front door to show the Johnsons when they got back.

Mr. Johnson had had to wear his tennis shoes to work the next day.

That was one of the worst dog stories George had ever heard.

But then there was the time when Kate Hinson's dog, Willie, was a puppy. Kate got Willie in the summer.

All summer Willie followed Kate everywhere. The first day of school he followed her to school. When Kate went into the school building she left Willie outside the front door. Willie barked for fifteen minutes. Then Willie found another way in. As Kate sat in opening assembly, she saw Willie walk right across the stage! George could still remember the way Kate's face had looked when the principal called out "Whose dog is this?"

Dogs could cause a lot of trouble. George had to keep Lucky from doing anything else bad. Today was his last chance.

He could imagine his father pointing toward the door. "That dog's out of control! That dog's got to go!"

George ran into the house. In the hall by the front door was a small puddle. Lucky had come in this way.

He had to find him fast!

He searched the living room.

No Lucky, but one more puddle. Lucky had come through here.

He searched the dining room.

Yes puddle. No Lucky.

Lucky could be anywhere. He had to find him. He also had to clean up those puddles before his mother found them.

George ran to the kitchen for a roll of paper towels.

As he hurried into the kitchen he thought of all the places that Lucky could be. In his room upstairs, in his parents' room, in his parents' closet, outside in the neighbor's yard, in the street!

There were so many possible places. How could he ever find Lucky?

He sighed. He had better get started.

George picked up the roll of paper towels and turned to leave the kitchen. As he turned, something caught his eye.

Something small and furry.

Lucky! He was curled tight in a ball, sound asleep in front of the refrigerator.

Lucky opened his eyes and looked up at George. He stretched out his front legs and yawned a big yawn.

Thump, thump went his tail.

With a sigh of relief, George sat down on the floor beside Lucky. He laid his head against the refrigerator door and said a small prayer of thanks.

He had found Lucky before he had been able to get into *too* much trouble.

Then he added another small prayer: Please let Lucky learn to behave himself.

Dog Looks

Lucky had found the most wonderful spot in the entire house, in front of the refrigerator.

It was perfect.

Warm air blew out of the bottom and warmed up the floor. The smells of the kitchen were great. Best of all the people were here.

His doghouse was too lonely.

He decided that he would sleep here from now on.

The boy had found him. He stretched up his chin so that the boy could pet him better. The boy scratched his neck.

The boy had more to learn about dog scratching. Sometimes he scratched the fur backward.

And he didn't scratch enough behind the ears. Behind the ears was the most wonderful of all scratching spots.

Still, the boy was coming along fine.

Lucky listened to the people talking in the kitchen. He was trying to learn what the words meant.

He had learned the good words first—*dinner, car, walk, treat, ham*, and the best words, *GOOD DOG*.

When he heard the words *GOOD DOG*, it meant that the people were about to pet him and give him treats.

He had also learned some bad words—*vacuum, doghouse, out*, and the worst words, *BAD DOG*.

When he heard the words *BAD DOG*, it meant that the people were about to hit him on the backside with a rolled-up newspaper.

It was helpful to know the language.

He lay beside the refrigerator, listening to the boy and his mother. He was hoping to hear some of the good words.

They kept talking. Most of the words he didn't understand. But finally he did hear a good one.

Car.

They were going somewhere in the car!

Dog heaven!

He loved the car. They went wonderful places in the car. They let him hang his head out the window. The air felt good on his face when they drove fast.

But would they take him?

The boy left and went upstairs. The woman cleaned up the kitchen.

He had to get them to take him along.

He thought back to what his mother had taught him. He remembered the lesson about dog looks.

There were three kinds of dog looks. All three were important. All three were useful.

The first was the "I can't believe it" look. To do this one you stared at your people. You looked at them as if you could not believe their bad manners. It shamed them into giving you what you wanted. Lucky's mother had learned this look from a French poodle.

The second was the "I am pitiful" look. This look was used to avoid punishment. For this look you made yourself look pathetic. People felt sorry for you and did not punish you. Lucky's mother learned this one from a golden retriever.

The last and most effective look was the "I can't wait" look. For this look you pretended that you thought the people were already going to let you do whatever it was that you wanted to do and that you were uncontrollably excited.

When the people saw how excited you were they just couldn't let you down. Lucky's mother learned this look from a cocker spaniel.

Lucky decided to use the "I can't wait" look. He moved to the back door and practiced.

One important thing about all the looks was never to look away first. You had to keep staring until you got what you wanted.

The *most* important thing about the looks was *never* to blink. If you blinked all was lost.

He got ready to use the "I can't wait" look.

When he used this look he always trembled a little and wagged his tail with all his might. Then even if they were not planning to take him they would change their minds. They would feel guilty if they left him behind when they saw his "I can't wait" look.

He heard them coming. He got ready. He shifted his weight back and forth from one paw to the other and wiggled his body. He stared his hardest right at the boy and . . .

It worked!

The boy picked him up. They headed toward the car.

He wiggled with delight. He had done it. He was going in the car with the people. His look had worked.

Now, where were they going, anyway?

As they got into the car Lucky heard the boy say a new word and he wondered what it meant.

The new word was *vet*.

Vet!

George held Lucky in his lap as they drove to the vet's office. Lucky looked happy. He had his nose poked out the car window. The air was blowing all over his face.

George petted him on the back. He felt a little guilty taking Lucky to the vet's after Lucky had been so excited about going with them. Lucky wasn't going to enjoy getting a rabies shot.

As they drove along George thought about the puddle problem. He had to train Lucky not to make puddles in the house. He had to train Lucky today. But how?

Maybe he could learn something at the vet about dog training. It was just about his last hope.

They pulled into the parking lot. The vet's office was in a little shopping center. George's mother was going to the grocery store while George took Lucky to get his shot.

"Do you need anything for Lucky at the store?" his mother asked.

George thought for a moment. They were getting low on puppy food. But after today they might not have a puppy anymore, anyway.

Maybe some dog biscuits would help train Lucky. He remembered the dog on television balancing the dog biscuit on his nose.

"Could you get him some dog biscuits?" he asked.

"Sure," said his mother. She headed toward the grocery store.

George hooked a long red leash to Lucky's collar.

Lucky scratched at the collar with his paw.

George picked Lucky up and put him down in the parking lot.

"Come," he said. He began to walk toward the vet's office.

Jerk.

The leash jerked tight. Lucky was not moving.

"*Come!*" George said louder. He thought that maybe Lucky had not heard him. He began to walk forward again.

Jerk.

Lucky would not budge.

People in the parking lot stopped to watch. George's face felt hot.

Now George knew that Lucky did hear him. He was just being stubborn.

George would have to show him who the master was.

"Come!" he said again and walked forward. Lucky lay down on the pavement. George dragged him. A few feet later, he stopped.

A small boy clapped for Lucky.

George walked back to Lucky.

"When I say come, you are supposed to come," he said.

Thump, thump went Lucky's tail.

A lady walked out of the vet's office with a big

black cat in her arms. They stopped to watch George and Lucky.

George tried one more time.

"*Come!*" he said.

Lucky rolled over on his back.

The people laughed and clapped.

George marched back to Lucky and reached down. Lucky looked up. He rolled over and sat up at attention.

He was not looking at George. His body was tense. The hair stood up on his back. He growled a puppy growl.

George saw the black cat.

The woman with the black cat saw Lucky growling. She began to hurry toward her car.

Lucky took off.

George had no idea how strong a puppy could be.

Lucky pulled George across the parking lot.

George could hear the people laugh and cheer.

Lucky ran until he got to the lady's car. The woman closed the door just in time.

Lucky gave one last bark at the cat when the lady drove away. Then he sat down and looked up at George.

Thump, thump went his tail.

George looked down at Lucky. Lucky was staring at him. He looked . . . pitiful. How could he punish him when he looked so pathetic? George sighed.

"Show's over, Lucky," George said. He picked Lucky up and carried him across the parking lot to the vet's office.

The vet was his last hope for training Lucky. His week was up and Lucky was out of control.

Rabies Shot

Lucky wagged his tail as the boy carried him across the parking lot.

He had just taught the boy something else. He didn't like the thing the boy called *the leash*.

They walked through a door. The boy was taking him somewhere new. It must be a wonderful place. It smelled like dogs and cats. This must be what they called the *vet*.

He wished the boy would put him down so that he could sniff around a little.

A man came out. He looked nice. He took Lucky from the boy. "What have we here?" he asked.

He scratched Lucky behind the ears right on

the special scratching spot. He knew exactly where to scratch dogs. Lucky could tell that this was a man who knew a lot about dogs. This *was* a wonderful place.

The man carried him into a room and put him down on a small red table. Lucky sniffed the table. He didn't like the smell of the table. It smelled like soap.

The boy held him on the table.

Lucky was curious. He listened to the man and the boy talk. What could they be talking about?

Maybe the man was teaching the boy!

Lucky hoped so. The boy had a lot to learn about dogs!

Maybe the man would show the boy the special scratching spot.

Lucky decided that *vet* was a good word.

Lucky watched some more.

The man picked up something shiny and turned to Lucky.

Lucky heard another new word.

Rabies-shot.

Before Lucky had time to wonder whether *rabies-shot* was a good word or a bad word, he found out.

AAAAOOOO!

Rabies-shot was definitely a *bad* word.

His hip stung on the spot where the vet had given him his shot.

He didn't like this place anymore. He wanted to go home.

He gave the boy his "I am pitiful" look. He hoped it would make the boy take him home. He trembled a little, and this time it was not an act.

It didn't work.

The man picked him up and walked away from the boy. He said another new word.

Flea-dip.

As they walked into the next room, the smell of soap got stronger and stronger.

Lucky had the feeling that he was about to learn the meaning of the worst word yet.

The Good Dog Book

While Lucky went back for his flea dip, George went out to the waiting room. It would take a little while to get Lucky dipped and dried off.

He picked up a catalog from the table beside his chair. He looked at the cover. THE DOG SHOP was written on the front. He looked inside.

On the first page was a set of matching sweaters with college emblems on them. One size for dogs, one size for people. A bulldog was modeling the dog's sweater.

On the next page was an advertisement for a dog car seat and a dog life preserver. George couldn't believe the things they made for dogs.

There was a set of dog rubber boots for rainy

days. Four boots, of course. There was a Frisbee that smelled like ham—

AAAAOOOOO!

He heard a wail from the back of the vet's office. It sounded like Lucky had just been dipped. Soon George could take him home.

George closed the catalog and put it back on the table. He looked across the room and saw a rack of books for sale. One title caught his attention.

The Good Dog Book.

George hurried across the room and picked up the book. He looked through the table of contents.

"Picking a New Puppy"

"Training Your New Puppy"

"What a New Puppy Must Learn"

It looked good, but would it help with the puddles? He read further.

"Teaching Your Dog to Come"

"Correcting Bad Habits"

"Puddle Problems"

George didn't need to read any more. This was the right book for Lucky.

This dog was about to get trained!

He put the book down on the checkout counter. He would ask his mother if they could get it when she came in to pay.

The vet brought Lucky out.

He was still wet from his flea dip. His hair was slick and damp against his skin. A few drops of water dripped from the tips of his ears. He rolled his eyes up at George and trembled.

When George took him from the vet, Lucky put his head down on George's shoulder and closed his eyes.

George carried him out to the car.

His mother was loading the groceries into the back of the station wagon.

"It looks like he's tired out," his mother said. "He's had a tough morning."

He's had a tough morning, thought George, What about *me*?

George could not remember ever having a tougher morning.

George put Lucky down on the backseat. Lucky curled into a tight ball and went right to sleep.

"Let's go pay the vet," said his mother.

George remembered the book. "Mom, there's a book I need. It's for sale in the vet's office, *The Good Dog Book*."

George's mother smiled. "Sounds like something we could use. Come in with me and we'll take a look at it."

"What about Lucky?" George said.

They looked at Lucky sleeping on the backseat.

"He'll be fine," said George's mother. "It's cool out here and we'll be only one minute. What trouble could he possibly get into in one minute?"

George took one more look at Lucky.

He hoped his mother was right.

Ham!

Lucky lay on the seat of the car, dreaming about good things to eat. He had tried a lot of good things in his life—hot dogs, a bite of roast beef, cheddar cheese. And once he had tried HAM!

All these wonderful things floated in and out of his dream. When he got to the part of the dream about ham, his feet kicked out and he let out a little puppy bark.

Ham was his favorite thing in the whole world. Into his dream came the smell of . . . HAM. It was a wonderful dream. When he woke up he could still smell the ham.

Sniff. Sniff.

He sniffed the air. Now he was wide awake. This was no dream.

Somewhere, somewhere near was HAM.

Sniff. Sniff.

Lucky began to sniff the seat of the car.

Not there.

He sniffed the floor of the car.

Not there.

He began to panic. Where was it!

He put his paws up on the back of the seat and looked over. In the back of the station wagon he could see some brown paper bags.

Sniff. Sniff.

Yes, the delicious smell seemed to be coming from the direction of the brown bags.

He began to jump up and down against the back of the seat. If only he could jump high enough, he could get over the seat to the bags.

Jump.

He fell back. He couldn't quite make it.

Jump.

He tried again, a little higher this time but no go.

Jump. Climb.

This time he learned to dig his claws into the back of the seat and he could almost *climb* over the seat.

Jump. Climb.

Closer this time.

JUMP. CLIMB. OVER!

He made it! Now to find the ham.

Sniff. Sniff.

He sniffed each of the brown bags. He could tell by the smell what was in each one, but he tore each one open just to make sure that he didn't miss the ham.

Cheese.

Milk.

Uh-oh, more dry puppy food.

Soap!

Finally, HAM!

He scratched the brown paper with his paws until a little hole appeared in the bag. The smell was stronger now.

Lucky's mouth began to water.

He could see the HAM!

But it was covered with something shiny and tough.

He began to dig at the plastic. It was stronger than the paper. It would not give way.

He tried his teeth. He chewed hard at the tough plastic wrapper.

He was desperate now. The smell was so strong.

He chewed harder and . . .

His mouth filled with the wonderful taste of ham juice. One of his teeth had punctured the wrapper.

He sat back and licked his lips.

Dog heaven!

Now he had a small hole to work with. He could chew and make it bigger and bigger and bigger . . .

That Dog

"BAD DOG!"

George heard his mother yell before he saw what had happened. He stepped up on the bumper of the station wagon to peer into the back window.

Lucky was lying in the middle of torn grocery bags, chewing on something. Groceries were scattered everywhere.

At the sound of George's mother's voice, Lucky jerked his head up. He cowered in the back of the car.

Worse than that, he began to make a puddle! Was this the end?

George's mother fumbled with her car keys.

The harder she tried to open the lock, the more her hand shook.

"That dog!" she said angrily. "That dog!"

The key finally slipped into the slot and the back of the station wagon opened.

George climbed in and tried to get Lucky out. Lucky ran back and forth in the back of the car. George slipped in the puddle.

Every time he tried to grab Lucky, Lucky would jump away. A bag of rice broke open and the rice flew in all directions.

George's mother just stood and watched, her hands on her hips.

Finally Lucky lay down and stared up at George. George looked down at the puppy stare. This time George did not feel at all sorry for Lucky.

He grabbed Lucky and pushed him to the side.

He found a roll of paper towels that his mother had bought. He opened the roll and pulled off three towels. He began to blot up the puddle.

Lucky began to lick George all over his face.

George pushed Lucky away and began to pick up the spilt groceries.

George's mother's mouth was in a tight line.

"That dog is out of control!" she said. "If you don't make him mind soon, he is going to have to go!"

Lucky looked at her and cocked his head to the side. George looked at her and began to work faster.

He finished his work and put Lucky over into the backseat. Then George crawled over the seat to the middle and buckled his seat belt.

His mother was right. Lucky *was* out of control.

But why was Lucky out of control? George had tried to be the perfect master. Where had he gone wrong?

He held Lucky in his lap and buried his face in Lucky's back.

George's mother got in the car and slammed the door. George could tell that she was angry.

A tear fell down on Lucky's soft back. Lucky turned and tried to lick George's tears away.

It was too late, George thought.

Maybe his parents were right. Dogs were a lot of trouble.

It seemed hopeless.

He looked down at Lucky. This was probably his last day here. Tomorrow they would take him back to the pound.

He would miss him.

When they got home, George took Lucky to the doghouse and put on the chain.

ERF! ERF!

George heard Lucky bark as he walked away. But this time he did not turn around.

ERF! ERF!

He kept walking toward the house.

Lucky had let him down.

He remembered the book that they had bought only an hour ago. *The Good Dog Book.* He had been hopeful then. Hopeful that he could train Lucky.

He wondered if it was too late. He wondered if he could ever train Lucky.

He took the book up to his bedroom and opened it. He turned to the chapter that he had been reading in the vet's office.

"Teaching Your Dog to Come"

He began to read.

> Put a long leash on your puppy's collar. Walk a few steps away, turn to face your puppy, and drop to a kneeling position.
>
> Hold out your hand and say "COME!" in an encouraging voice. As you give the command, jerk forward on the leash.
>
> If your dog comes toward you, reward him with your praise and pats. You can also give him a food reward.
>
> Remember at all times to show your dog who is in control.

George thought about that. When had he lost control of Lucky? Had he ever had control of Lucky?

He thought about the morning, his embarrassment in the parking lot, the torn grocery bags in the car, the puddles in the house.

A dog out of control made an unhappy master.

He thought about taking Lucky back to the pound.

A dog out of control made an unhappy dog too.

Maybe being a good master meant more than just pats and saying "good dog." That hadn't worked at all. Maybe being a good master meant getting your dog under control.

George would not give up without a fight. Even if Lucky did have to go, he would try to teach him this one thing. He would teach him to come.

He put the book down and picked up the red leash.

He felt like the sheriff he had seen in a movie. The sheriff in the movie had a showdown at dawn. He had marched out into the main street of the town to do battle with the outlaw. The sheriff and the outlaw had faced each other in the street eyeball to eyeball. Then the battle had begun.

George hitched up his jeans as he had seen the sheriff do in the movie and headed downstairs.

The time had come. It was time for a showdown.

Showdown

Lucky sat in his doghouse. He couldn't believe that the boy had left him all alone.

What was the problem, anyway? These people just didn't understand dogs. Dogs have instincts. Dogs like ham.

ERF! ERF!

He called the boy again.

How can I ever train the boy if he leaves me out here all alone?

ERF! ERF! *AAAAAOOOOO!*

Still the boy did not come.

Lucky put his head down on his paws. The boy was not coming this time.

He tried to go to sleep. He remembered the ham in the grocery bag. He remembered the wonderful smell of the ham. He remembered the wonderful taste of the ham juice in his mouth.

His stomach growled. In all the excitement they had forgotten to give him lunch.

He heard a noise. Someone was coming. He looked up and saw the boy walking across the yard toward him.

Lucky wagged his tail.

They had remembered his lunch! They had finally realized that he belonged in the house with them! They—

He stopped wagging his tail and looked closer at the boy. The boy had the long red leash in one hand. In the other he had some dog biscuits.

He was happy to see the dog biscuits, but what was the leash for? Hadn't he already shown the boy that he hated the leash? Hadn't he sat down firmly and made the boy pull him last time?

That should have been proof enough that he didn't like leashes.

So now what was the boy going to do with that leash?

George walked up to the doghouse and took off the chain. Then he attached the long leash to Lucky's collar.

I won't budge, thought Lucky, no matter what, I won't budge.

He stared at the boy. He used his "I can't believe it" look. The boy stared back.

They stared right into each other's eyes for a full minute. Lucky blinked.

The boy took the other end of the leash and walked away.

When the leash was straight and tight, he stopped and turned around and looked at Lucky.

No matter what, I will not budge, thought Lucky.

"Come!" the boy said.

Come? There was that word again. What did it mean?

Right now Lucky didn't care what it meant. He was concentrating too hard on the bad feeling of the leash attached to his collar.

"Come!" the boy said again. This time the boy jerked the leash toward him.

Jerk!

The collar cut into Lucky's neck and pulled him down into the grass.

It hurt a little.

What was the boy doing?

"Come!" the boy called again.

Lucky began to back up. He pulled at the collar and arched his back against the leash like a bucking bronco.

I will not budge, he thought.

Jerk!

The boy pulled him forward again.

Down on the grass he went again.

Six times the boy said "Come," and six times the boy jerked the leash forward. Six times Lucky was pulled down onto the grass.

After the sixth time he looked up at the boy. He couldn't believe the boy was doing this to him. It looked as if the boy was getting ready to jerk the leash again.

This time, Lucky decided, he would try something different. This time when the boy said "Come," he would trick the boy. Instead of letting the boy jerk him forward into the grass, he would run forward *toward* the boy. Then the boy could not jerk the leash and hurt him.

"Come!"

Lucky ran forward toward the boy. When the boy jerked the leash, Lucky kept running. He didn't even feel the jerk!

He had tricked the boy!

"GOOD DOG!" the boy yelled.

Good dog?

The boy was *happy*?

Lucky loved to make the boy happy. He loved to hear the boy say those magic words *good dog*.

He kept running toward the boy. When he got to the boy the boy petted him all over and gave him a dog biscuit and called him "GOOD DOG."

Now he knew what *come* meant! It meant I

have a dog biscuit for you, and I want to pat you, and I want to call you *good dog!*

Next time he heard the boy say "Come" he would run right to him!

What a wonderful master he had.

The Ten-foot Puddle

George petted Lucky over and over. He gave him another dog biscuit.

What a wonderful dog he had!

What a wonderful *book* he had.

Before today George had no idea just how useful a book could be. This one would help him save Lucky, he hoped.

George walked back away from Lucky and called him again.

"Come!" he said. Lucky did not even hesitate. He ran straight to George.

George called him over and over, and every time he called Lucky he came.

Lucky *could* learn something! He had learned to come!

Maybe there was hope for Lucky after all.

He took off the leash and rubbed Lucky on the neck. Lucky rolled over on his back. George scratched him on the chest.

Learning to come was an important thing, but right now it was not the most important thing. His father would be home soon and they had not made *any* progress on the puddle problem.

George remembered his book, *The Good Dog Book*. It had a chapter called "Puddle Problems."

He ran inside to get the book. Lucky followed him.

George hurried up to his bedroom and sat on the bed. Lucky sat down on the floor beside the bed.

He opened the book to the table of contents and quickly ran his finger down the list of chapters.

62

He turned to page 42 and began to read.

Whenever your puppy makes a puddle outside, give him a reward. The reward can be praise and pats.

Whenever your puppy makes a puddle indoors, show him that this is not allowed.

Puppies hate loud noises. One way of showing him would be with a string of cans. Each time you see your puppy begin to make a puddle indoors, throw the cans beside the puppy. The goal is not to hit the puppy with the cans but to make a loud noise beside the puppy. Say "bad dog" and quickly take the puppy outside.

A string of cans? Bad dog?

It didn't sound nice to George. It sounded cruel. But taking Lucky back to the pound would not be nice either.

He decided to try it. It wouldn't hurt Lucky, and it might work. The book had been right about "Teaching Your Dog to Come." Maybe it was right about puddles too.

He closed the book, stepped over Lucky, and ran down to the kitchen. He would start the training now. The puddle problem was going to be solved today, or else.

It didn't take long to find some cans and string. Within a few minutes George was ready.

He tried it out in the kitchen. He aimed for the kitchen rug and threw the cans.

CRASH! CLATTER! CLANG!

They made a lot of noise.

He hoped the noise would get Lucky's attention. He would go upstairs now and wait for Lucky to make a puddle.

When Lucky made a puddle he would be ready.

He knew the signal that Lucky was about to make a puddle. Lucky always sniffed a little, circled three times, then squatted.

When Lucky sniffed, circled three times, and squatted, George would know that it was time to throw the cans.

He picked up the cans and ran back up to his room. Lucky was still lying on the floor. He had found a baseball shoe and was chewing the toe.

George sat down on the bed and waited.

Lucky looked up from the shoe at George and tilted his head to the side.

George didn't smile. He waited and watched some more.

Lucky got up and walked out the door to the hall.

George followed. He never took his eyes off Lucky.

Lucky stopped at the end of the hall.

He sniffed a little. He circled once. George tightened his grip on the cans.

Lucky circled twice. George lifted up his throwing arm.

Lucky circled the last time and began to squat—

CRASH! CLATTER! CLANG!

The cans hit the floor beside Lucky.

George watched.

Lucky jumped a foot into the air. He took off running. When he took off running, he did *not* stop making the puddle.

He made a long, dribbling ten-foot puddle from the beginning to the end of the hall.

Lucky disappeared down the steps.

George didn't have time to worry about the puddle. George charged after him. He remembered the second part of the lesson. Scold him and take him outside quickly.

George caught him. He looked down at the trembling dog in his arms. He wanted to hug him and say, "It's okay, boy." But he didn't.

"BAD DOG!" he said instead. He took him out into the backyard and put him down. Lucky was still trembling a little. He sniffed. He circled three times, squatted, and finished his puddle.

"Good dog!" George said now. "Good dog."

He patted Lucky over and over again.

He hoped the book was right. The string of cans still seemed a little mean to George.

It did get Lucky's attention. But it had also

caused a ten-foot puddle in the upstairs hall.

He would keep trying the cans all afternoon. He didn't know how else to train Lucky.

He hoped it would work.

George picked up Lucky and headed back into the house. He had to go upstairs.

He needed his cans. And he had a ten-foot puddle to clean up.

Dog Heaven

Lucky sat beside the table with his head resting on his paws. His people were eating dinner. His people were eating HAM.

It had been a long afternoon.

These people just didn't know what dogs liked. All afternoon the boy had been throwing some terrible noisy thing called *cans* at him every time he made a puddle.

What was he supposed to do? How was he supposed to make puddles? He really had a puddle problem.

Worst of all, they still gave him only dry puppy food and kept all the good things for themselves.

The smell of ham coming from the table was unbearable. It made him weak with desire. He couldn't bear to watch them eating bite after bite of juicy, tender, delicious ham.

He followed every bite with his eyes. His head went back and forth as the bites of ham on the boy's fork went from his plate to his mouth.

Plate to mouth.

Plate to mouth.

As he watched, the boy picked up a small piece of ham from the edge of his plate. He said something to the woman. Lucky watched his every move. He could not take his eyes off the ham.

This time the boy did not eat the ham. This time the boy turned in his chair.

"Here, Lucky," he called.

Lucky couldn't believe his luck. The piece of ham was for *him!*

Lucky hurried over to the table and snapped at the piece of ham in the boy's hand.

The boy pulled his hand back.

"No!" he said.

No?

What kind of game was this? Was the boy going to give him the ham or not?

The boy held out the ham again, higher this time.

"Beg," the boy said.

Beg?

What did *beg* mean, Lucky wondered.

Lucky sat up on his hind legs to get a better smell of the ham.

As soon as he sat up on his hind legs, something wonderful happened!

"Good dog!" The boy said the magic words. Lucky didn't move. He kept sitting up on his hind legs.

The boy's hand came down and dropped the ham right into Lucky's mouth.

Dog heaven!

He had done it. He had trained the boy to give him the ham. Now he knew what to do.

"Beg," the boy said again, holding up another bite of ham.

Lucky sat up on his hind legs. He hoped the

boy would not forget what he had learned. He was supposed to give the piece of ham to Lucky.

The ham lowered.

Dog heaven again!

He had trained the boy! He had done it!

He tried again and again. Even the man and the woman were pleased. The man cut off another slice of ham for the boy to give Lucky.

Life just got a little better, thought Lucky as he ate bite after bite of the juicy ham.

Better, but not perfect. One thing still bothered Lucky. The puddle problem. How could he get the boy to stop throwing the cans at him?

If I could only solve the puddle problem, he thought. Then life would truly be perfect.

The Barking Problem

George felt great. He had trained Lucky to do two things in only one day.

Lucky had shown that he could learn to come. Lucky had shown that he could learn to beg. But he had made no progress on the most important thing. The puddle problem.

All day George had followed Lucky around with the cans.

Five times he had thrown the cans. Five throws, five puddles in the house. Lucky wasn't catching on at all.

He looked over at his father across the table. He was cutting another slice of ham for Lucky. He was laughing at Lucky.

Maybe his father was beginning to like Lucky.

Maybe this was the time to ask if he could keep Lucky. George gave it a try.

"Dad," George asked. "Do you think we can keep him?"

"Well," his father began. "We had a rough start. But I see that you have made some progress with him. How are we coming with the puddle problem?"

George didn't answer. The answer was "not good." The answer was "not good at all."

There was a moment of silence.

"I see," his father continued. "And how are we doing with the night barking? I heard him again last night."

George's throat felt tight. He had been so worried about the puddle problem that he had forgotten all about the barking problem. The book did not have a chapter on barking at night.

George couldn't sleep in the doghouse forever.

Was it hopeless?

He had an idea.

"Dad, do you think Lucky could sleep in the kitchen? I know he wouldn't bark if he slept in the kitchen."

His father frowned.

"Until the puddle problem is taken care of, that dog will have to sleep outside!"

He frowned again.

"If the puddle problem is not taken care of, that dog will have to go back to the pound!"

George was silent.

When his father started calling Lucky "that dog," it was time to stop the conversation.

George looked down at Lucky. Lucky was sitting up on his hind legs. He was looking up at George with his cutest stare.

George felt his eyes fill with tears.

He handed Lucky one more piece of ham.

Lucky had shown George that he could learn *some* things. But could he learn the two most *important* things?

People Training

Lucky looked at the boy and the man and the woman sitting around the table.

He had trained them to give him ham. How could he train them not to throw cans at him and yell "bad dog" every time he made a puddle?

He had to think of a way to teach them, fast. He needed to make a puddle right now!

Maybe he could just avoid the puddle problem altogether by making the puddles outside.

But how could he get out the door?

He had trained the people to give him ham. Maybe he could train them to open the door for him.

They seemed to be in a good training mood.

Lucky decided to give it a try.

He ran to the kitchen door to see what would happen.

He barked once.

The boy jumped up from the table. The woman jumped up. The man jumped up.

"GOOD DOG!" they all three yelled together. Then all three ran toward the door.

Did they ever get excited!

"GOOD DOG!" they yelled over and over.

If he had known how excited these people would get over his barking at the door, he would have done it a long time ago!

The man opened the door.

Lucky ran outside, sniffed, circled three times, and made a puddle in the grass.

They went wild again! GOOD DOG!

These people sure were easy to train!

The man ran back inside the house and brought out—more HAM!

They petted Lucky over and over.

Lucky marched proudly back into the house.

At last he had trained his people! He had solved the puddle problem.

It was easy after all.

He decided that he would bark at the door and make puddles outside from now on.

It would be one way to keep the people from throwing cans and yelling "bad dog!"

It would be a good way to keep these people trained to open the door and say "good dog."

Lucky lay down in front of the refrigerator. Everything seemed perfect. He closed his eyes.

He was tired.

Training people was hard work.

He was content. He was in his favorite spot. He was in the house. His stomach was full of warm ham. And the words *good dog* still echoed in his brain.

He drifted off to sleep. No need to bark tonight.

Good Dog

George and his mother and father gazed down at the little dog sleeping in front of the refrigerator. For a moment they were silent.

George's parents looked at each other in agreement.

His father was the first to speak.

"George," he said, "I think we have quite a good dog here. You have come a long way with him in only a week. I'm proud of you."

George smiled. He was proud of himself. Training Lucky had been hard, maybe the hardest thing he had ever done.

Lucky was well on his way to learning to be a

good dog, and George was well on his way to learning to be a good master.

His father had said that he had come a long way. Was it enough? Did this mean he could keep Lucky?

Before he could ask, his father continued.

"It would be a shame not to keep Lucky now that his training is off to such a good start."

KEEP LUCKY!

His dad had said the words "Keep Lucky."

He smiled his biggest smile at his mother and father. His parents smiled back.

"Thanks, Dad! Thanks, Mom!" George said. He hugged his father, then his mother, then his father again, then his mother again.

"I'll keep working with him. I'll keep him under control."

George bent down and scratched Lucky behind his ears. Lucky was his dog now.

He watched him sleeping.

In a few minutes he would have to take him out to the doghouse.

He scratched him again.

Lucky slept soundly, but his back legs kicked out in a little puppy kick at the pleasant feeling of the scratch.

George wished that he could leave him there.

His parents started to walk away. Then his father turned back.

"Oh, George," he said. "Lucky looks so content. Let's let him sleep where he is tonight."

George smiled again.

The barking problem had just been solved! If Lucky slept inside he wouldn't bark.

George leaned back against the refrigerator. Now everything seemed perfect. He closed his eyes.

He was tired.

Training dogs was hard work.

It was his bedtime too. Tonight he could sleep in his own bed. Tonight there would be no barking.

He gave Lucky one more scratch behind the ears and stood up.

Before he went upstairs to bed, he watched Lucky sleeping for one more minute.

Then he bent down and whispered two words softly in Lucky's ear. The two words that are the happiest words for a dog to hear and the happiest words for a master to say: "Good dog."

About the author

Betsy Duffey was born in Anderson, South Carolina, and attended Clemson University. *A Boy in the Doghouse* is her second book for children. The character Lucky is derived from Ms. Duffey's experiences with her puppy, Chester, and the ten other dogs she and her family have owned over the years.

Betsy Duffey lives in Atlanta, Georgia, with her husband and two sons.

About the illustrator

Leslie Morrill has illustrated many books for children. He lives in Madison, Connecticut.